All That Is Solid

Rosanne Rabinowitz

All That Is Solid by Rosanne Rabinowitz

ISBN: 978-1-908125-93-4

Cover Art by David Rix

Publication Date: October 2019

All text copyright 2019 Rosanne Rabinowitz

All That Is Solid originally appeared in The Scarlet Soul: Stories
for Dorian Gray, edited by Mark Valentine and published by
Swan River Press in 2017.

Just before she goes out, Gosia takes down *Worst Case Scenario Survival Tips*. It was a gift from an old colleague, and they're all having a reunion drink tonight. She'll bring it with her. They can have a laugh about it. Or something.

The book offers advice on how to jump from a bridge into a river. How to wrestle with an alligator or escape a rabid wolf. How to escape underwater bondage or quicksand. How to fend off a shark. *Hit it in the eyes!*

Philippe had written: 'To a beautiful future for us all!'

The magazine they'd been launching folded after three issues but they'd already scattered to other projects. Gosia barely remembers the magazine's content, though she had enjoyed the graphics work.

Once she opens the book, it's hard to just close it and put it in her bag. All joking aside, she sees herself in it. That's her, always ready for the worst. Around every corner, an abyss yawns. Sod's law rules: whatever can go wrong will go wrong.

Just in case, she needs to know:

How to escape from killer bees.

How to perform a tracheotomy.

How to land a plane.

But the most important worst-case scenario is missing: what do you do when you might be uprooted from the country where you've lived most of your adult life?

She'd been looking forward to this little reunion, arranged after several months of negotiation and schedule-juggling in true cat-herding fashion.

But as the group huddles in a corner of the crowded bar, her mind wanders to her worries again. When they were all working together, she'd been so excited to be living in a new country, speaking the language she'd studied for years, doing her first design job. But what's become of that now?

She tunes back into the conversation. They're still trying to stop talking about the referendum result. Again.

Philippe asks: "Remember when Remedy Double wasn't a cliché?" There's a desperate gaiety in his voice.

"Yes, Remedy Double was new and bold. A top font!" They clink glasses for no good reason.

The old dread seizes her: jagged glass scraping at her insides, scooping out a void at the centre of her body. *Atoms, space. Nothing there.*

The anxiety used to be constant, but things got better. She made friends, found jobs. Calmed down. Found lovers too.

"Yesterday someone told me to go back to where I come from because Brexit won," Sunil is saying.

Well, that didn't take long . . . back to Brexit after a full three minutes of chit-chat about fonts!

"I was in Islington at the time, so I said, yeah, sure, I'll take the tube back to Southwark to see my mum. That's where I come from."

He adds: "Then I made a quick exit before the geezer could punch me. He was pulling his beefy arm back and all . . ."

They give up after that. Might as well let that elephant in the room take its rightful place, sitting and pooping at the centre of the table.

Gosia leaves her friends to catch her bus.

Worst case scenario, she thinks: I twist my ankle while I'm crossing the road and get hit by a car.

Or perhaps I meet that alligator. Wandering up Drury Lane, as alligators do.

Rule Britannia, Britannia rules the waves . . . " A chorus of drunken voices sings out behind her.

You don't expect to hear that among the theatres and bars of Covent Garden.

Every hair on her body stands up in a grim salute. Stray alligators are likely to be the least of her problems.

"First we'll get the Poles out, then the gays!"

Her heart starts rushing in a build-up to full-throttle panic. She walks faster. She can't look back. Can't run. No, don't run.

Rule Britannia . . . There it goes again, the hateful refrain.

First we'll get the Poles, then we get the gays.

She ends up at the busy bus stop on Kingsway in front of a Wetherspoons. But that's the chain with the Brexit beer mats. She's sure people are nodding, smiling in agreement. *First we get the Poles out.*

She turns and walks, keeps walking over Waterloo Bridge. Then she runs.

She's sweating when she reaches the South Bank. She feels sick. She scolds herself for it. Can't even have a drink with friends. You'll turn so miserable, you'll drive everyone away, even Ilona. You'll fuck up. You'll get deported. Everything will unravel.

○

As Ilona listens to Gosia, she thinks about neighbours. There are neighbours that blast out your most despised genre of music, or engage in theatrically vocal and thumping sex in the bedroom just above yours.

And there are the neighbours she's just been reading about. After years of civility, they put excrement through letterboxes and leave notes saying it's 'time to leave'.

So far she hasn't faced that problem, not when her upstairs neighbour is Gosia, who has just given her lunch.

And she also sees that Gosia has hardly touched her own portion.

"I keep thinking of horrible things happening, over and over," says Gosia. "I can't concentrate. All I do is worry, worry, worry."

"Just because you have an anxiety disorder doesn't mean there's nothing to worry about," Ilona says.

"Great!" Gosia spears a piece of beetroot in emphasis, then lets it fall off her fork.

"What I mean is that you're not *wrong* to worry. I'd be shitting myself too if those guys were singing that song behind me. Even though I'm technically German rather than Polish. You probably wouldn't remember that Leipzig, my home town, was called the City of Heroes because we had the first demonstrations that led to the fall of the Wall. But I'm no hero . . . who is? It's normal to be afraid."

"Well, I never knew it was a *thing*. It was just . . . 'you worry too much'. Now I hear it's a *disorder*, an anxiety *disorder*. Whatever you call it, I'd give *anything* to get rid of it. To be free."

Ilona is disturbed by the fervour in Gosia's voice. She speaks as if she's ready to get a knife and cut a piece out of herself.

But she comes across this all the time, working with artists. She's really a bloody *bookkeeper*, not a shrink. And she knows where this conversation must go. "We do face a threat, of course. But there's a kind of worry that just makes it worse. And then there's worrying about worrying and things that are not related at all."

"Like atoms. Fucking atoms," Gosia mutters.

"Atoms? You mean, like nukes? I used to worry about that too. You're younger than me, so you wouldn't remember much about the Cold War. But I'll tell you about the fear that went with it. We thought the West was going to bomb us. I was *convinced*. Then I grew up and we became part of 'the West', and I met people from the other side who'd been afraid of the same thing."

"No, it's not that," says Gosia. "It's this obsession I had when I was a kid. I learned about atoms and space. I started to freak out because it meant that nothing is solid, everything is made up of spinning atoms and *space*. It's weird, I know."

"'All that is solid melts into air . . .'" Ilona makes quote marks with her fingers.

"That's terrible. What are you saying?"

"Karl Marx said it. Didn't you read the *Communist Manifesto* in school? You must've done that in Poland, my cousins did."

But of course not, Ilona thinks. Lucky girl, she's too young. The Cold War, the Wall, reading Marx in school ...

"No, that was before my time," Gosia confirms. "And you know, even when I was a hardcore activist, I didn't read it. What did I want with books by dead old men with beards? I just wanted to fight fascists."

This makes Ilona feel even older, perhaps older than Karl himself.

And now it's time to make her suggestion and hand out the number of that sensible therapist, known to be woo-woo and psychobabble-free.

○

Gosia looks at the crayons and paper in front of her. Is this what it's come to . . . playing with crayons?

"Draw a picture of your anxiety. Draw as many pictures as you like. I've got lots of paper," says Sophie the therapist. She's a plump, comfy woman with the barest trace of a Manchester accent. Ilona was right. Sophie doesn't do psychobabble. However, Gosia is apprehensive about drawing.

She picks up a black crayon and holds it above the paper. "I studied some art, along with English literature," she says. "This seems like a joke."

Sophie nods. "Makes it more difficult, doesn't it? You'll get that inner critic jabbering at you. Tell it to shut the fuck up."

Gosia laughs. She doesn't expect a therapist to say 'fuck'.

"But I don't draw any more. I do design on a computer," she says as she makes random circular scribbles with the crayon.

Then she recognises what she's drawn. Barbed wire, tearing at her insides. She adds red but dulls it. Rust, not blood. This wire hasn't drawn actual blood. But it will. Then she encloses her marks with more wire. This wire shines like new stainless steel. The silver-coloured crayon does its job.

Gosia adds some pale green, thinking of broken glass at the back of her throat.

She leans back, exhausted. And she realises she can breathe without that scrape of worry. She can think without the refrain: *something bad is gonna happen.*

Gosia leaves Sophie's flat with the drawing rolled up in a carrier bag, along with a set of crayons. She stops to buy more paper, thick cream-coloured A3.

For the first time in weeks, she's aware that a summer evening can be pleasant. The heat made the traffic fumes especially stomach-turning but now she enjoys the warmth.

She walks through a little square near Elephant and Castle where houses now go for millions. Mulberry trees stand in the middle, their twisted branches supported by stilts. She's amazed that the trees are full of actual berries. Their ripe scent reaches her as she walks underneath. She stops to pick and taste. She'd expect London berries to be dusty and sour. Instead, they're sweet and luscious.

She picks a bunch of berries and puts them in the carrier bag with the drawing.

When she gets home she unfurls her drawing and sticks it up on the living room wall with Blu-Tack. It's been spattered by mulberry juice, as if someone's been killed.

She chuckles as she retrieves the remaining mulberries from the carrier bag and gives them a rinse before popping a few in her mouth. Then she takes a beer out of the fridge and puts the news on.

A Polish man has been attacked and killed . . .

That moment of feeling okay, even good, fades.

Here she is in the front room of *her* flat on the top floor of a solid Georgian house. She'd bought it when homes in this area were cheap. Her flat with thick walls and high ceilings had been a bargain, just about affordable for a precarious if skilled freelancer like her.

But now those solid walls shimmer and fold in front of her eyes.

In school, she learned that *everything* is made of atoms, and these atoms have space between them and contain space inside them. So even solid things are filled with emptiness. She found that idea frightening. If she put her foot down, it could go through the floor and she'd fall into a hole.

No floor under her feet, no real roof to keep the rain and wind away.

Everything she's done or built fragments into the thick summer haze. *All that is solid melts into air.*

Who is she? What is she? Where will she be next year or the year after that?

What did Sophie suggest? Set aside an hour a day for worrying. Then don't worry the rest of the time. Think of what she's doing, looking at a sunset or eating mulberries.

But she's watching the news and worrying. Watching the floors and walls of her home dissolve. Atoms, just atoms. Space between, space inside. Places to fall.

When she was a child, these thoughts kept her up at night. She'd pat her bed, making sure it was still there. She woke screaming from dreams of falling. Or worse, she'd be unable to make a sound.

Her parents contacted her science teacher and they all had a chat. The teacher said these distances are so tiny, you can't even see them. Don't worry about them. "You'll have plenty of real things to fret about when you're older," he added.

Under this persuasion, the worries about atoms faded. In fact, she didn't do badly in science at all. She liked biology.

But other concerns came along.

Worries about things she said, things that *he* said. The grades on papers.

Speaking to people.

She dared herself to defy these fears. She became the best shoplifter in her home town – only got caught once. And she still did well in school.

She hitched around the world, fended off attacks. Lived in squats and fought the police. She wrestled with the anxiety demon inside her and very often she won.

Now all the things that once bothered her are fading into insignificance. It's worse than it's ever been. Overnight she's been declared foreign and unwanted. Her home is threatened, the ground beneath her feet has shifted. The space between the atoms yawns, the electrons whirl around a see-through nucleus that is ready to explode. Any day.

Draw the worry . . . again. And what does that corrosive, helpless anger *look* like? Drawing those negative feelings made her feel so much better. It wore off but she can replenish it. She can try.

Gosia scribbles on a fresh piece of paper.

What do you feel?

She's cut up. Barbed wire. She's choked with it, scratched and scraped from the inside. It spreads in her stomach, uncoils against her skull. Twisty and tangled, black barbed wire. More wire, silver like a blade.

If everything's made of atoms with space inside them and it's all about to come apart, can't the barbed wire come apart too?

I would do anything to get rid of that feeling, she said to Ilona the other day. I would give anything. She said that to Sophie too.

What could she give?

This mess of a picture lacks something. It needs to be much more of a mess.

She knows what's missing. More red, scarlet red. Deep red drying to brown, the colour of blood.

She cuts her finger. It's only a little. But when she adds a few drops, the picture looks just right. It makes sense. It makes her relax.

Then she walks on the street and watches people as they pass. The mother with two little boys. The man with the walking stick who smiles at her when he meets her eye. Would he smile if he knew where she's from? Is he one of the people who voted to force her from her home?

So she takes out her crayons and crafts the curls of barbed wire that scrape inside her. It brings the gratification of an itch receiving a scratch. There's a moment of dizziness, as if the ground beneath her feet has shifted. But surely it's only the shrinking of space within its atoms – enough to make her feel safe for a while.

○

When Ilona calls on Gosia, she's puzzled by her friend's behaviour. Gosia's cheeks are flushed, her eyes intent. She ushers Ilona into flat without a word, her walk weaving as if she's drunk or disoriented.

"Sorry, did I interrupt something?" Ilona asks. "I'll come up later."

She braces herself, as if expecting to see a carved-up body. Perhaps Gosia tracked down one of those oafs from the other night. Maybe she learned to do things like that in her Antifa days.

"No, come in. I'd like you to see this. I've just been doing some art therapy. And know what? I think it's working."

She sees that Gosia had pulled the extensions out on her table and it's covered with drawings. Other drawings are on the wall.

Art therapy? It's art, full stop. Made with basic materials, but look at it! Barbed wire – black and grey and silver, some old and rusted, some gleaming. Flakes of red.

It looks alive, as if something vital runs through that wire. Jagged veins of iron, filled with unknown substances. She's not sure it would be blood.

There's something very *wrong* about it. She's looking at more than a collection of images, but the product of some profound violation. It makes her stomach flip over, her core shrivel.

But with the way things are now, shouldn't art be unsettling?

"Gosia, this is fantastic." She means it even though her skin is crawling. "You're a real artist! Do more of this, it might be just what you need. Was it Sophie's idea?"

"She got me started. But I think this is all mine, for better or worse. But don't talk *bollocks* about me being an artist." Gosia is emphatic in her use of mild British profanity. She smiles. "That's *bollocks*. I do *graphics*, not art."

"Whatever . . ." Ilona looks at the drawings again.

Yes, that wire must have a living force trapped within it. It is vital in the way a cancer is vital, filled with a life that consumes life.

Maybe Gosia does need to get out more.

Later, Ilona suggests that they go on an anti-Brexit demonstration, a March for Europe. She has to do some persuading, which doesn't seem right. Usually Gosia is the one up for a demo.

You'd expect that, given her background – and Ilona's own past. What was she doing in the City of Heroes in 1989?

When the weekly demonstrations in Leipzig started, she stayed in because she was worrying about whether she'd get into art school if she was seen there. She had bowed out when history was being made, playing it safe for art or ambition or an easier life.

○

A noisy crowd is filling Park Lane. So many signs sport *I love EU* and other puns about 'you' and 'EU', so many faces are painted blue with circles of stars. Ilona has never felt such affection for the EU itself. But she couldn't imagine life without it, or a life outside of the one she has made for herself in London.

"These stately and slow walks can get dull," says Gosia. "Not like the old fash-fighting days."

Ilona shrugs. "I don't mind a relaxed ramble for a cause myself. And there's a good selection of placards."

Most look homemade and brightly painted, a display of thought, effort and emotion. They express sentiments that comfort her: *Don't deport my neighbour. No borders, no Boris! Brexshit. Sick of this shit.*

A woman with deep blue hair and a gold tiara of stars on top of it holds up a sign: *'Homeland' is wherever we live, wherever we work.*

She's walking alongside a bicycle-pulled sound system. Written on its side: *The world is my country, all people are my brethren, to do good is my religion. – Tom Paine.*

The boom of dance music starts up. Ilona and Gosia follow the sound and the blue beacon of the woman's hair and end up in front of a pub on Whitehall where a dancing crowd is gathering.

Gosia beams and she waves to someone in the crowd who bears a placard that says *Here is home.* Oh, it's that nice French boy from her old job. Then Gosia is waving at someone else as she joins the dancing.

Ilona wishes that she could bump into her old friends too. Someone she works with, perhaps, or another neighbour. No chance of that though. She thinks she's content enough just to watch the younger people dance.

○

After the demo, Gosia isn't doing so much drawing. She means to ring Sophie to arrange another appointment, but maybe she doesn't need therapy. She takes her worst-case scenarios book out of her bag at last. Maybe she'll get rid of it. Philippe won't know.

She was at first squeamish about all the star-spangled blue body art and *I love EU* puns at the demo. After all, she must have demonstrated *against* the EU several times, concerned about policing and austerity; the exclusion of those from outside Europe. But she understands now that the other demonstrators have been declaring their love for their European friends, neighbours and partners rather than politicians in Brussels.

What's there to worry about?

She's looking forward to some free time between jobs. Time for DIY, picking more mulberries, or a trip to the seaside. Check out a gig.

Before she goes anywhere, she rings to confirm when she's expected for her next job. It's a regular assignment with one of her favourite clients, a fusty but friendly bimonthly heritage magazine.

Gosia doesn't recognise the voice that answers her on the phone. Sounds young and bubbly, perhaps she's a temp.

"Gosia here, the designer. Have you set the production schedule? When should I come in?"

A muffled sound of conferring in the background, a clearing throat: "Sorry, we've decided to use an in-house designer. The budget for freelancers has been cut so one of our subs has been trained up to do the job."

The voice at the other end of the phone drips with treacle.

Acid fills Gosia's throat, dissolving the words that are trapped there.

Now she's thrown back on herself and her own resources. What happens when she can't make the mortgage payments? Will she even be able to sign on? And Working Tax Credit is already on its way out.

She gets out the drawings again. Never mind Sophie. She might not be able to afford more therapy, but at least she knows what she can try at home.

She adds convolutions to the barbed wire. New borders have already been drawn, cutting her down the middle. Not too long ago she had crossed the hard but shifting border between those who have and those who don't. Her younger relatives won't even see that frontier.

She could add the demonstration, where people declared their will to dissolve these borders. *Wherever I live and work is my homeland.* People dancing that declaration. She can't write those words out in thick crayon, but she can show their colours. First, the green of the forests and farmland she knew as a child. But it also becomes the colour of grass in the park where she goes to sit and watch the cranes swinging over Elephant and Castle.

Deep red, like the mulberries in the square;

brighter red, like a London bus. The scarlet haze that fills her head when she's angry and there's nowhere for it to go.

She tints grey with yellow, the sun through London clouds.

She can now breathe again without razors shredding from inside; the acid flooding her mouth is gone.

She goes to the shop for milk, and picks up biscuits and a piece of brie. As she's waiting to pay, she glances at the newspapers displayed near the cash register:

Shopkeeper flees as arsonists strike Romanian food shop.

A photo of charred, unrecognisable items on the pavement outside.

She hurries home. When she returns, the splashes of colour that had pleased her so much look like tatters of clothing caught on the wire.

○

Ilona opens the door to find Gosia brandishing a bottle of wine. "Need some time out of the flat," she says. "That thing I made is getting creepy."

"Come in, then. I was just watching TV. The wine is very welcome!"

She's surprised by such a visit. Usually she goes upstairs to chat and unwind within the colourful chaos of Gosia's flat. She prefers her own place to be *just so*. She's accumulated beautiful things over the years, and each should have its proper place.

Ilona watches Gosia negotiate her way past the *objets d'art* in the corridor, nearly knocking over a reasonable facsimile of a Grayson Perry urn. She sets the urn straight, settles at the kitchen table. "It's work," Gosia begins. "Or *not* working . . ."

Ilona's own job with a large arts charity is secure – she *believes* – yet so often she has envied Gosia's more free-wheeling risk-taking life.

"Guess freelancing isn't so free after all," she remarks. "But haven't you had droughts of work before?"

"Yes . . ." says Gosia. "But this made me suspicious. Like some new arse-wipe of a manager said 'shouldn't we have *British* people working on a magazine about British heritage sites?'"

"Anyone can write about a building," sniffs Ilona. "I can't believe that a specialist publication would be so stupid."

"And when I went to the shop, I saw a headline in a paper that scared the shit out of me. A Romanian shop in Norwich . . ." Gosia shudders.

"Yes, I read about that. And I also read an update on the internet. Have you? All the neighbours came out in force to help, and there's been donations from all over the city."

"That's . . . good. But why did that firebombing happen in the first place?"

"So one, two, a few people threw that firebomb. But many more people pitched in to help the shop owner."

"Yes, I can imagine them chanting . . . Pierogi, yes! Bigots, no!"

"Bigos?" Ilona deliberately confuses *bigot* with the meaty Polish stew. All those 'you' and 'EU' jokes must've put her in a punning mood. "Nothing wrong with *bigos*! Of course, vegetarians might object to it."

Instead of laughing as she should, Gosia turns pale. "I've just realised . . . My job for next month involves designing pamphlets for the EU statistics bureau. My client has been running that contract for three years. I've not considered that it would end. There's so much none of us have considered."

"So . . . what's for you to worry about? You're an EU citizen."

"But I do it through a UK firm that will lose the contract. And I lose the work."

"Listen, Gosia, I think large helpings of pierogi and bigos will do us both good."

○

Off they go to the Pierogi Palace, a café-bar that features Polish beer, vodka and food. The gorgeous grub fills Ilona with nostalgia as well as carbs, invoking memories of the hostel in the mountains near Zakopane where her family stayed every year. Ilona is glad to see that Gosia has her appetite back .

They usually speak English with each other, but under the influence, they slip into Polish. Ilona's out of practice at first, even though she grew up speaking Polish with her cousins. She sees Gosia smiling at her rather stilted German-inflected speech.

However, it's the pierogi that sparks the most disagreement after their meal. As they get on the bus, they're both in a merry mood after several bottles of Perla, plus shots of Zubrowka and Roza vodka. They go upstairs and sit at the front so they can watch the streets of their city go by.

"I steered clear of that newfangled pierogi," says Ilona. "Goat's cheese and kale? No thanks!"

"Things must change," says Gosia. "You can't live in the past. Life changes. So does our pierogi."

"You're talking philosophy, not dumplings. Yes, we must move on. But must I like goat's cheese and kale pierogi to be forward-looking?

And there's worse – I saw black truffle pierogi on a menu. Cost a bomb. It's *criminal* to charge so much for proper peoples' food – it's a gentrification of the stomach!"

They clutch each other as they laugh. Gosia pats her stomach, comfortably rounded with their hearty meal. "Well, gentrify this!"

More people are getting on. The air is now thick with the scent of alcohol and sweat, despite their open window.

A thump to the back of their seat. "You're in England, so speak English!"

"Polish bitches have to leave now, don't you."

Gosia is frozen, stock still as if blinded by headlights. "This isn't in my worst case scenario book," she whispers. "We should ignore them." She looks ahead with blank eyes and a wan little smile that isn't her at all.

Another kick to their seat.

Gosia's reaction shocks Ilona as much as the attack. This is her friend who once fought fascist skinheads, police, or both – adding to Polish Antifa's formidable reputation. She's done so many things that Ilona had always been too timid to do.

Then she's angry, so angry at forces that have broken her friend's spirit. Despite the drunken fun earlier in the evening, she now seems lost. A shell.

"The fuck I'll ignore them!" Ilona turns around to confront their tormenters.

One fat guy with a red face. One skinny guy with a weasel face. A girl, kind of pretty. But pretty is as pretty does . . .

"Look at you!" Ilona screams. "Are you the master race? Look at the state of you!" She holds up her phone and takes rapid photos. "Bastard bigots with shit for brains . . . you're on YouTube now, how do you like that?"

Everyone else on the bus is just watching.

The skinny guy's hand snakes out and he makes a grab for Ilona's phone. She yanks it away just in time and slaps his face with her other hand. It's not a very good slap, but he stares at her as he rubs his face. He's shocked at her action.

And she's surprised too. She's never been one for fighting.

"Give him another one, lady!"

"Yeah, leave those girls alone!"

"You can't hit my mate! You ain't no lady, you're an ugly Polish slag!"

"My granddad lived here and worked and he can't get nothing . . ."

You think anyone's handed me anything?

"You'll get a punch in the face if you don't leave 'em alone!"

"Fat Polish slags!"

"Skinny little dickshit!"

Someone's got the big guy in a chokehold, while a woman aims a punch at his stomach.

And the thin bigot is about to take a whack at her.

The bus pulls over and stops, the driver's up the stairs and striding forward. "No fighting, no fighting – get off my bus or I call the police," he commands. "Anyone who is fighting, get off the bus!"

"We'll get them off . . . They were bothering the two ladies up front."

"Get off! Get off!" Half the bus is chanting at the attackers.

But what about the other half?

◉

Gosia declines Ilona's invitation for more vodka in her flat. "But thanks for standing up to the bullies. I just quivered in my seat. I don't know what got into me."

"Don't worry about it. It was nothing. Don't fret now. How about brunch tomorrow? I'll make a frittata. With goat's cheese and kale!"

"Yes, that'll be great. I'll have the coffee ready."

As soon as Gosia closes the door to her flat, those last shots of Roza threaten to come up. You can't find Roza in London shops, and she enjoyed those shots so much. But now their aftertaste feels like a sickening syrup in her mouth.

Gosia is disgusted at her spinelessness. She's been drained of her will to fight.

She really thought she was feeling better after she drew the wire that was scraping out her insides. Now she wonders if she has also drawn out the wire that held up her backbone, and unravelled her very veins.

Then she knows what she must do. She'll still have to deal with her anxiety later. But at least she'll get her spine back.

She puts on some music and spreads her drawings out. They served their purpose, now they've done too much for her. Too much *to* her.

Always mindful of health and safety, she remembers that she has a metal bin – a housewarming present from the ever-practical Ilona. It's still in the cupboard. She gets it out and places it near the sink. She fills up a bucket for any emergency dousing needs.

She puts the first of the drawings in the bin and brings out her lighter. She flicks it a few times. She hasn't had much use for it since she gave up smoking.

"Thank you, Sophie," she says. "But I don't think I'll make another appointment."

This time the lighter works. She doesn't feel anything as the paper catches fire. An artist would feel sad to watch her work go up in flames, but there's not even a twinge. They were only crude sketches anyway, just *therapy*.

The taste of iron floods her mouth and spreads upwards into her mind. Cold steel flexes her fingers, stiffens her legs. Nothing can hurt her.

Ilona pauses by the door. She hears music. She knocks. Once, twice . . . a third time.

So maybe Gosia has popped out to the shops.

Ilona takes her key out and opens the door, shouting for Gosia in case she's in the flat. No answer.

Music's still on. It was playing last night. After that fracas on the bus, no wonder the poor thing couldn't sleep.

"Gosia! Gosia!" she calls again. "Are you ready for brunch? Shall I bring the frittata up?"

She sniffs the air. Something smells funny. A burnt smell. Definitely not coffee.

She flings open the door to the front room.

A bank of barbed wire extends across it, a barrier twisting and curling in thorny loops. It gleams so thick and black. There are scraps of clothing mounted on it. Ilona recognises pieces of

Gosia's socks, a mixture of dusted magenta and rose. A scrap of lace, somehow poignant. Pieces of other material decorate the wire as well. They come in different colours – deep green, a juicy mulberry colour, scarlet.

This work says so much. The barbed wire, a border running through the artist's own home. Gosia is so self-deprecating. *Just* a graphic artist, she says.

Well, Ilona knows of a few places that could be interested in this installation. That'll cheer her up.

The singed smell comes from the kitchen, but there's no sign of a fire.

Ilona struggles to move some of the wire aside and manages to get through to the kitchen. Must've been an experiment, Ilona thinks when she sees ashes and burnt papers in the bin near the sink. Gosia had been worried about some scientific issues – atoms, space, whatever.

She makes a pot of coffee in preparation for her friend's return. After half an hour she rings Gosia.

And a phone rings from the kitchen. That must be Gosia's phone.

Worry stabs at her. Why did she leave her phone?

No, no . . . Nothing unusual about that. Who wants a phone call when you're buying a pint of milk?

But as time wears on, Ilona is sure that something terrible has happened.

She'll wait a while, then start ringing Gosia's friends on that phone of hers.

She picks up a newspaper, but puts it down straight away. The news is all bad.

Then she finds that 'worst-case scenarios' book Gosia loves to quote from, hanging on a hook of wire. She removes it, but she can't bear to look at it. Instead, she chucks it into the bin with the ashes of Gosia's 'experiment'. She knows it's meant to be funny, but it can't do anyone with an anxiety condition any good.

She spots a sheaf of blank papers and crayons near the sink.

Gosia did say that Sophie's art therapy seemed to be working. Perhaps she should give it a try while she waits.

Ilona makes some marks on the paper. Ah, she feels better already.

Just wait. Gosia will walk in the door and she'll make another coffee.

Rosanne Rabinowitz started writing when she produced zines in the 1990s such as *Feminaxe* and *Bad Attitude*, contributing articles, reviews and interviews. Then she began to make stuff up... Her debut fiction collection *Resonance & Revolt* was shortlisted for the British Fantasy Award and her earlier novella *Helen's Story* received a nomination for the Shirley Jackson Award. Recent tales have appeared in anthologies such as *Uncertainties III, Murder Ballads* and *Pareidolia*.

Rosanne lives in South London, an area that Arthur Machen once described as "shapeless, unmeaning, dreary, dismal beyond words". In this most unshapen place, she works at several occupations including care work, copywriting and freelance editing – and recovers with whisky, chocolate, strong coffee and loud music.